Land of NOW

Activity Kit

Contents

Land of NOW Activity Kit

Text and Illustrations Copyright 2020 Faceted Press®

ISBN: 978-1-947459-50-2

Published by Faceted Press®, a division of Faceted Works, LLC.

Printed in the United States of America
by Kindle Direct Publishing

Book design by Faceted Press®.
The Yabbut® and Land of... Children's Books®
are trademarks of Faceted Press®.

For information, fun resources,
and free downloads visit
www.LandofChildrensBooks.com/fun-stuff/

Land ᵒᶠ NOW

How to Be Present and in the NOW

Here are some ways to help you stay in Land of NOW
and enjoy the NOW, the only moment we truly have.

Sit here in NOW; in this Land you will find
Ways to clear all the chaos and quiet your mind.

- NOT in the NOW -

"Even though we're both here in the very same place,
Sharing this very same spot,

Your view of the NOW is unruly and wild
Thanks to your unending thoughts."

The first thing you must do to be in the moment is to recognize when you aren't in the NOW, when your thoughts have taken over.

Are you paying full attention to what is happening around you? Do you remember the conversation you just had with someone? Are you feeling anxious or sad, or even frustrated and unwilling to accept what is happening around you?

If so, then you AREN'T in the NOW. Start paying attention to your thoughts and where they are dragging you off to.

- Not in the NOW -

Activity

What are some things that you miss out on when you aren't focused on them or in the NOW?

_____

_____

_____

_____

_____

_____

_____

_____

List some simple things to bring yourself back to NOW, like wiggling your toes.

_____

_____

_____

_____

_____

_____

The NOW
Guide & Kid

When you find yourself not in the NOW, remember us and join us in the NOW to be in the present, the only moment we really have.

- Thoughts of All Things -

"Yeah but these thoughts… don't I need all of them?"
I blurted so very confused.

"'Cuz I'm always thinking. My brain's always full.
Don't ALL of my thoughts have a use?"

Yes, we think that we need ALL of the thoughts that are rambling around in our heads. But the truth is, just because the thought showed up (to take us out of NOW) doesn't mean that it's useful.

In fact, if you really listen to the thoughts you are having, you will realize that most of them don't have a use – other than to fill your brain with useless, meaningless babble.

And know that the Yabbut is trying to get you to listen to all of those thoughts, and convince you that you need them, all of them.

- Thoughts of All Things -

Activity

Print a sheet for everyone in the family. Each time you hear "yeah but" from that person about why they are **hanging on to useless thoughts and not in the NOW**, mark it on the sheet.

Count the Yabbuts!

Name: _____

- Hear Your Thoughts -

"To uncover the NOW and get rid of this ruckus
You need to stay quiet and hear

Each of the thoughts that you're constantly having
And let them begin to appear."

As you begin to realize that you are stuck in your thoughts, and not in the NOW, take a moment to hear what is happening in your head.

When our thoughts are in charge, what we usually experience is this constant background noise of chatter, bouncing from one topic to the next, doing nothing but distracting us from the NOW.

Listen to your thoughts as if they were someone else talking at you. Let them become separate from one another, and from you. As you do this, you become the observer that is hearing them.

- Hear Your Thoughts -

Activity

Listen to the thoughts that are running amok in your head. What are they saying? Write them down. Are these thoughts really you? Or, are you the one hearing the thoughts?

_____

_____

_____

_____

_____

_____

_____

_____

_____

_____

_____

_____

_____

_____

_____

_____

_____

_____

_____

_____

_____

_____

- Fretters of the Future -

"The first thoughts I saw looming there in the haze
Brought with them worry and fret.

They made me quite nervous of what was to come,
Of a future that wasn't here yet."

Is it the future that is causing you to not be in the NOW because you are worrying about a time that isn't even here yet?

Do these future thoughts offer a plan or something that you can do NOW to affect the future? If so, then take those steps NOW to help get rid of those worries. If not, then please understand that since there is nothing you can do about it in this moment, worrying does you no good. Just take what is useful and can be applied to the NOW, then let the future thoughts move on.

Talk about your future worries. When you point them out, they lose power. Ask yourself if what you are really worried about is even true.

– Fretters of the Future –

Activity

What are you worried about? Is the worry a real thing? Can you do anything about it here in the NOW? If so, what?

What are you worried about? _____

Is the worry something real?_____

If so, can you make a plan or do something about in the NOW?_____

_____

What are you worried about? _____

Is the worry something real?_____

If so, can you make a plan or do something about in the NOW?_____

_____

What are you worried about? _____

Is the worry something real?_____

If so, can you make a plan or do something about in the NOW?_____

_____

What are you worried about? _____

Is the worry something real?_____

If so, can you make a plan or do something about in the NOW?_____

_____

Future Thinklings

We are the thinklings of your Future Worries and Frets. But are we real or not? Is there something you can actually do in the NOW to make sure that we don't happen?

- Pesterings of the Past -

"The next thoughts that appeared were of things from my past,
Like errors that still caused regret.

And ways I was treated that still made me mad.
All these times I could just not forget."

Does the past still gnaw at you, causing sorrow or anger over what happened or how you behaved? Do these thoughts keep you from the NOW?

Well, the past is over and you cannot go back to change what occurred. But, you keep that pain alive by thinking about it.

If you are still angry about how someone else treated you, you need to let it go by forgiving them. I guarantee you they don't even remember. The only person you hurt is YOU by holding on to the past. If you are mad at yourself for the way you behaved or what you did, forgive yourself.

– Pesterings of the Past –

Activity

List the things that you regret doing or saying. What can you learn from them? How can you do things differently next time?

What you regret doing: _____

What you can do different next time: _____

What you regret doing: _____

What you can do different next time: _____

What you regret doing: _____

What you can do different next time: _____

What you regret doing: _____

What you can do different next time: _____

What you regret doing: _____

What you can do different next time: _____

What you regret doing: _____

What you can do different next time: _____

What you regret doing: _____

What you can do different next time: _____

What you regret doing: _____

What you can do different next time: _____

Past Thinklings

We are the thinklings of your Past Regrets. We love it when you think about us because it keeps us around. But we will go away when you are in the NOW.

- Resisters of What IS -

"The last of these thoughts that were blocking the NOW
Were insisting that things should all shift.

They wanted it their way; to change what was fact,
And did not like What IS and were miffed."

Another BIG way we keep ourselves from the NOW is when we don't want to accept What IS.

If you are spending time thinking about how you don't like this, or don't like that, or wish things were different, then you are not in the NOW. When you go against What IS, you only cause yourself more pain and frustration.

If there is something YOU can actually do to make things better NOW, then do it. Don't just complain about What IS. Also, try and be grateful for what REALLY is and all that you actually have.

- Resisters of What IS -

Activity

List the things you are grateful for that you have here, in the NOW. Once you start to list some things, more of them appear. Think about these things every day. This is the easiest way to enjoy the NOW.

_____

_____

_____

_____

_____

_____

_____

_____

_____

_____

_____

_____

_____

_____

_____

_____

What IS Thinklings

We want things to be different. But, when you think about all that you have NOW, you help us enjoy the moment as well, and appreciate What IS.

- The Never-Ending NOW -

"You see, my dear friend, you are always in NOW
So please do not waste one more minute

Being stuck in your thoughts, missing out on what's here.
The NOW's all there is so be in it."

The good news is that NOW is always with us, but we can easily be pulled out of the present.

So if you find that you are feeling worried, upset, or have missed out on what just happened, then you aren't in the NOW, and your useless thinking has come back.

But returning to the NOW can be as simple as taking a big deep breath in, and feel the air fill your lungs. Or, just notice something around you, in the NOW.

Focus on the music you hear playing, or notice the wind blowing the leaves outside, or even just stretch your fingers. All of these simple activities can help you come back to NOW.

- The Never-Ending NOW -

Activity

What are some ways that you can bring yourself back to the NOW? How can you remind yourself to always **Be Here NOW**?

_____

_____

_____

_____

_____

_____

_____

_____

_____

_____

_____

_____

_____

_____

_____

_____

_____

_____

_____

_____

_____

_____

To learn more about being present and staying in
Land of NOW, visit www.LandofChildrensBooks.com
Art and Text © Faceted Press®

Word Finder

How many words can you find from Land of NOW

```
J  W  B  S  L  V  N  D  E  F  C  Q  Z  N  D  W  Z  M  J  C
K  O  R  M  M  Y  H  T  P  Q  X  N  C  O  B  N  F  E  L  C
J  Q  T  T  S  B  C  R  I  U  Q  K  B  H  Q  A  U  W  I  Z
T  P  I  H  W  O  R  R  I  E  S  O  V  K  P  Y  N  C  L  F
W  G  Y  B  E  D  J  E  G  K  A  Z  S  Z  P  T  R  A  Q  X
H  S  T  B  L  R  V  U  D  A  Q  K  Z  W  R  S  I  Y  E  S
U  I  T  H  P  S  W  J  S  D  W  L  A  E  X  B  Z  A  F
L  Z  J  H  O  G  N  I  K  N  I  H  T  P  S  Z  R  C  P  H
A  A  E  P  G  S  Y  A  W  L  A  L  U  F  E  T  A  R  G  T
O  N  V  W  I  U  S  T  E  R  G  E  R  T  N  E  M  O  M  S
B  Y  Q  J  N  Q  O  S  A  S  W  B  N  P  T  M  P  G  E  A
Y  I  C  U  O  D  S  H  T  L  T  A  Y  V  F  I  H  Q  P  P
V  R  Y  C  N  O  R  Q  T  B  L  B  A  U  R  A  A  J  N  V
D  L  E  I  N  U  T  U  E  P  M  X  B  M  V  N  L  A  S  O
T  M  M  S  R  Y  W  W  N  S  H  Z  B  C  T  P  E  C  C  A
S  Z  E  N  N  G  X  S  T  F  E  R  U  T  U  F  N  U  E  J
A  M  S  O  A  H  C  J  I  F  I  B  T  Z  B  T  D  H  W  G
B  X  A  W  A  R  E  F  O  R  G  I  V  E  Y  N  N  S  F  I
I  A  V  M  M  C  F  D  N  S  D  Z  I  H  E  J  V  O  R  J
F  B  N  U  R  D  N  J  B  Z  Z  T  Z  R  F  K  D  U  W  B
```

NOW	PRESENT	MOMENT
THOUGHTS	MIND	YABBUT
THINKING	FUTURE	WORRIES
PLAN	PAST	REGRETS
LESSONS	ACCEPT	FORGIVE
GRATEFUL	CHAOS	ATTENTION
ALWAYS	AWARE	OTHER

Land ^{of} NOW
Word Finder Key

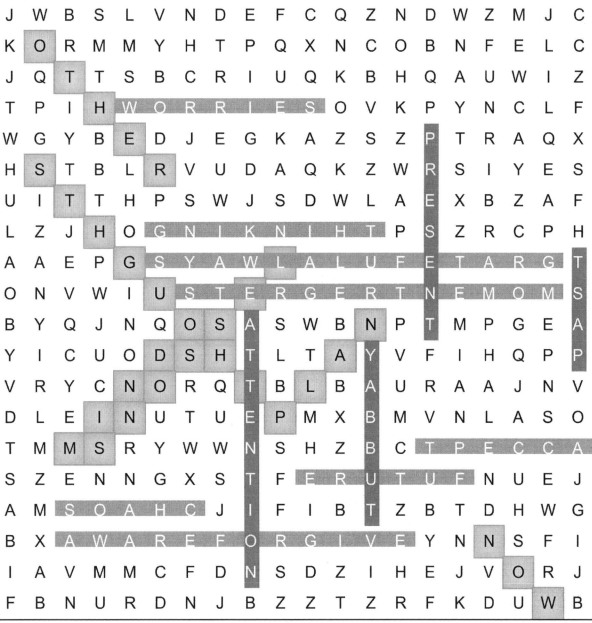

J	W	B	S	L	V	N	D	E	F	C	Q	Z	N	D	W	Z	M	J	C
K	O	R	M	M	Y	H	T	P	Q	X	N	C	O	B	N	F	E	L	C
J	Q	T	T	S	B	C	R	I	U	Q	K	B	H	Q	A	U	W	I	Z
T	P	I	H	W	O	R	R	I	E	S	O	V	K	P	Y	N	C	L	F
W	G	Y	B	E	D	J	E	G	K	A	Z	S	Z	P	T	R	A	Q	X
H	S	T	B	L	R	V	U	D	A	Q	K	Z	W	R	S	I	Y	E	S
U	I	T	T	H	P	S	W	J	S	D	W	L	A	E	X	B	Z	A	F
L	Z	J	H	O	G	N	I	K	N	I	H	T	P	S	Z	R	C	P	H
A	A	E	P	G	S	Y	A	W	L	A	L	U	F	E	T	A	R	G	T
O	N	V	W	I	U	S	T	E	R	G	E	R	T	N	E	M	O	M	S
B	Y	Q	J	N	Q	O	S	A	S	W	B	N	P	T	M	P	G	E	A
Y	I	C	U	O	D	S	H	L	T	A	Y	V	F	I	H	Q	P	P
V	R	Y	C	N	O	R	Q	T	B	L	B	A	U	R	A	A	J	N	V
D	L	E	I	N	U	T	U	E	P	M	X	B	M	V	N	L	A	S	O
T	M	M	S	R	Y	W	W	N	S	H	Z	B	C	T	P	E	C	C	A
S	Z	E	N	N	G	X	S	T	F	R	U	T	U	F	N	U	E	J
A	M	S	O	A	H	C	J	I	F	I	B	T	Z	B	T	D	H	W	G
B	X	A	W	A	R	E	F	O	R	G	I	V	E	Y	N	N	S	F	I
I	A	V	M	M	C	F	D	N	S	D	Z	I	H	E	J	V	O	R	J
F	B	N	U	R	D	N	J	B	Z	Z	T	Z	R	F	K	D	U	W	B

NOW	PRESENT	MOMENT
THOUGHTS	MIND	YABBUT
THINKING	FUTURE	WORRIES
PLAN	PAST	REGRETS
LESSONS	ACCEPT	FORGIVE
GRATEFUL	CHAOS	ATTENTION
ALWAYS	AWARE	OTHER

Land of NOW
Finger Puppets!!!

To make these fun puppets, just follow these simple steps.

You will need:

CRAYONS

SCISSORS

TAPE

1 Print this PDF.

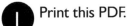

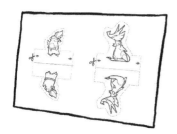

2 Color the puppets.

3 Cut along the dashed lines to cut out the puppets.

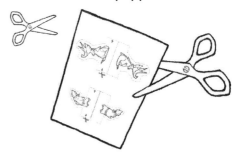

4 Fold each puppet in half along the black solid line.

5 Cut along the dotted lines.

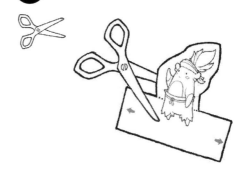

6 Roll the bottom into a tube so that the arrows touch; then tape it together. It should be a little bit bigger than your finger.

7 Hooray! You just made finger puppets!

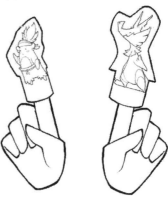

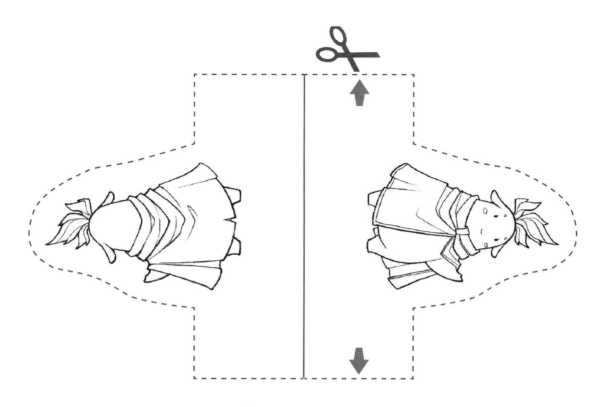

The Kid - YOU in Land of NOW

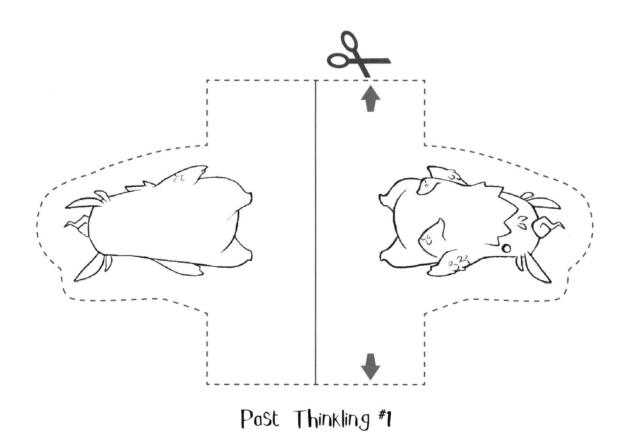

Past Thinkling #1

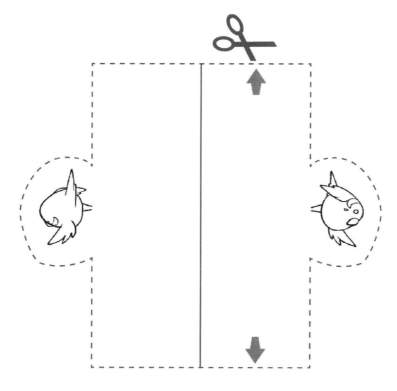

The Mynah Bird

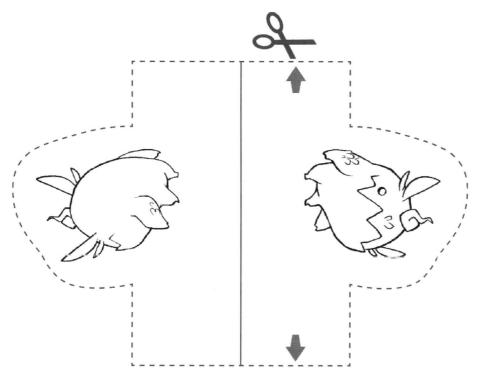

Past Thinkling #2

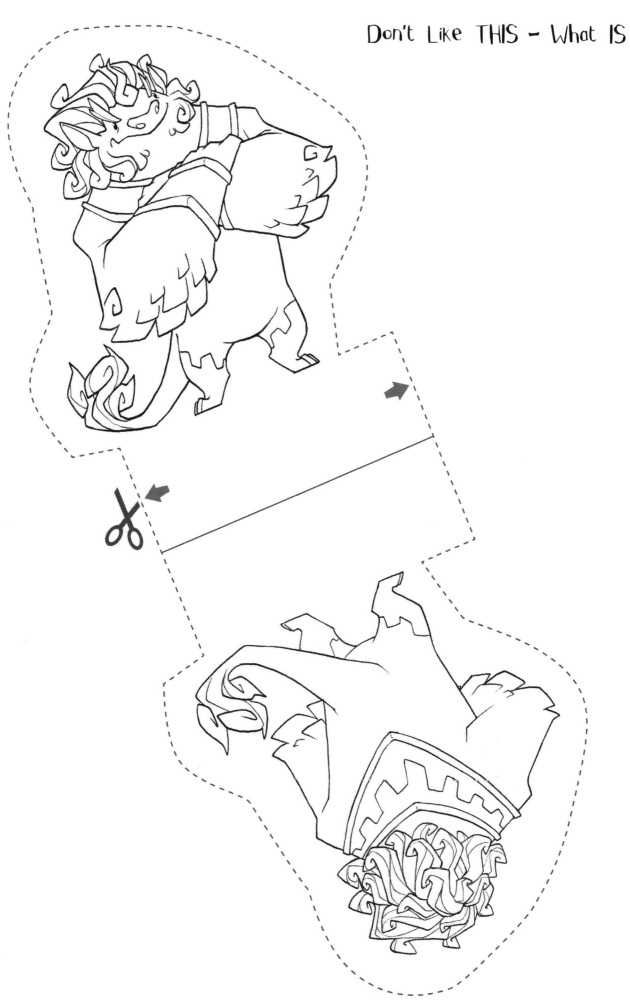

the Yabbut®

The Yabbut you see, it has only one use;
to always be near and provide an excuse.

Made in the USA
Middletown, DE
30 October 2022

13789010R00029